Ruth Wielockx

Luke and Lottie
and Their Vegetable Garden

Clavis
NEW YORK

Luke and Lottie are playing outside.
"Here it comes!" Luke yells. He kicks the ball hard.
The ball rolls far away. Luke and Lottie run after it.
"Look!" Luke shouts. "What a nice new sandbox!"

Lottie looks surprised. The sandbox is strange. The sand is so dark . . .
But Luke is already playing. He's building a sandcastle.
Suddenly they hear Dad. "Luke, that's not a sandbox!" he shouts.

"Then what is it?" Lottie asks curiously.
"I built a vegetable garden for you," Dad says.
Luke looks sad. "I ruined our vegetable garden," he says.

"It's okay," consoles Dad. "It was only dirt. I thought we could plant the vegetables together. Want to help?"
"Yes!" Luke and Lottie shout simultaneously.

Dad, Luke, and Lottie go to the garden center.
"Mm, it smells lovely in here," Lottie says.

"Should we get these flowers for Mom?" Luke asks sweetly.
"Sure," Dad smiles. "You can put them in the shopping cart."

"Look, Dad! An apple tree," Lottie says.
"You can grow all sorts of things in your garden," Dad explains.
"Vegetables, fruits, herbs, and even edible flowers."

Luke looks a bit worried:
"Is Mom going to eat our flowers?"
"No," Dad laughs. "Not all flowers are edible!"

"Here you can choose plants," says Dad.
He looks at the plant Lottie picks up. "That's a lettuce plant."
"Oh, I like this one! It's a little baby lettuce," Lottie laughs.
"I like radishes," Luke says, "Where are the radish plants?"
"Radishes grow from seeds. You have to sow them," Dad explains.
"Look, here's a packet of radish seeds."

When they get back home, Luke and Lottie get ready to garden.
"I put on coveralls," Luke says.
"And I put on my flower sweater," says Lottie.

Dad has set out the wheelbarrow.
In it are a rake, the plants, and vegetable seeds.
"Can you bring the watering can?" Luke asks.
"I've got it!" shouts Lottie.

First Lottie rakes the dirt. "This is where I'll put the baby lettuce," she points. She makes holes in the soil with her finger. Then she puts a lettuce plant in each hole.

"Now you have to press the dirt against the lettuce plant to make it firm," Luke says. He does the same with a strawberry plant.

"You can scatter radish seeds over here," says Dad.
"Just like you sprinkle sprinkles on a cupcake.
Then we'll cover the seeds with dirt."

Next Lottie puts the empty seed packet on a stick like a hat and she puts it in the right spot. That way they'll know which seeds were planted there. That's clever!

"Now we still have to press down the dirt," Lottie says wisely. "Otherwise, the seeds will wash away when we water the vegetable garden."

Then Luke says, "I'm going to plant a candy tree."
He puts a candy in the ground.
"A candy tree? That's not possible, Luke!" giggles Lottie.

Lottie waters the vegetable garden.
Luke is impatient. "I still don't see anything," he says.
Dad laughs. "You'll have to wait a little longer, Luke.
The plants need time to grow. You didn't grow big
in just one day, did you?

"I used to be a baby," Luke says. "But now I'm big.
And if I eat all our vegetables, I'll grow even bigger. This big!"
"But first clean your plate," laughs Mom. "Enjoy!"